FIRST EXPERIENCES

SAMMY'S FIRST SLEEPOVER

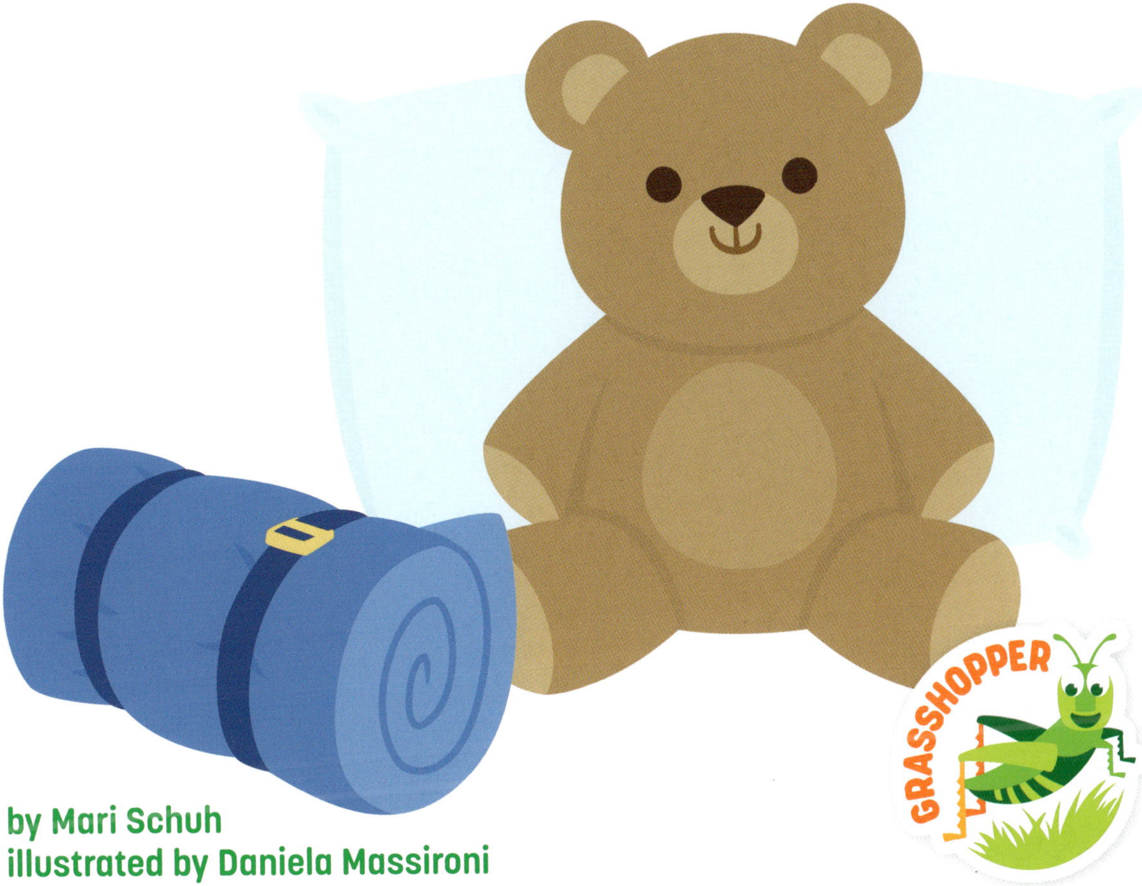

by Mari Schuh
illustrated by Daniela Massironi

Tools for Parents & Teachers

Grasshopper Books enhance imagination and introduce the earliest readers to fiction with fun storylines and illustrations. The easy-to-read text supports early reading experiences with repetitive sentence patterns and sight words.

Before Reading

- Look at the cover illustration. What do readers see? What do they think the book will be about?
- Look at the picture glossary together. Sound out the words. Ask readers to identify the first letter of each vocabulary word.

Read the Book

- "Walk" through the book, reading to or along with the reader. Point to the illustrations as you read.

After Reading

- Review the picture glossary again. Ask readers to locate the words in the text.
- Ask the reader: How did Sammy feel before the sleepover? How does he feel after? How do you know?

Grasshopper Books are published by Jump!
5357 Penn Avenue South
Minneapolis, MN 55419
www.jumplibrary.com

Copyright © 2023 Jump! International copyright reserved in all countries. No part of this book may be reproduced in any form without written permission from the publisher.

Library of Congress Cataloging-in-Publication Data

Names: Schuh, Mari C., 1975- author.
Massironi, Daniela, illustrator.
Title: Sammy's first sleepover / by Mari Schuh; illustrated by Daniela Massironi.
Description: Minneapolis, MN: Jump!, Inc., [2023]
Series: First experiences
Audience: Ages 4-7.
Identifiers: LCCN 2021059761 (print)
LCCN 2021059762 (ebook)
ISBN 9781636909363 (hardcover)
ISBN 9781636909370 (paperback)
ISBN 9781636909387 (ebook)
Subjects: LCSH: Readers (Primary)
Sleepovers–Juvenile fiction.
LCGFT: Readers (Publications)
Classification: LCC PE1119.2 .S377 2023 (print)
LCC PE1119.2 (ebook)
DDC 428.6/2–dc23/eng/20211216
LC record available at https://lccn.loc.gov/2021059761
LC ebook record available at https://lccn.loc.gov/2021059762

Editor: Jenna Gleisner
Direction and Layout: Anna Peterson
Illustrator: Daniela Massironi

Printed in the United States of America at Corporate Graphics in North Mankato, Minnesota.

Table of Contents

Away from Home 4
Let's Review! 16
Picture Glossary 16

Away from Home

"Are you excited for your first sleepover, Sammy?" Mom asks.

"Yes, but what if I miss home?" I ask.

"Let's pack your favorite toy," she says.

On the way, my tummy starts to hurt.

"What if I want to come home?" I ask.

"Call anytime. I will pick you up," Mom says.

We get to Ray's house.

I am happy to see my friend.

"Hi, Sammy!" Ray says.

Ray's dad makes pizza.

It is my favorite!

Yum!

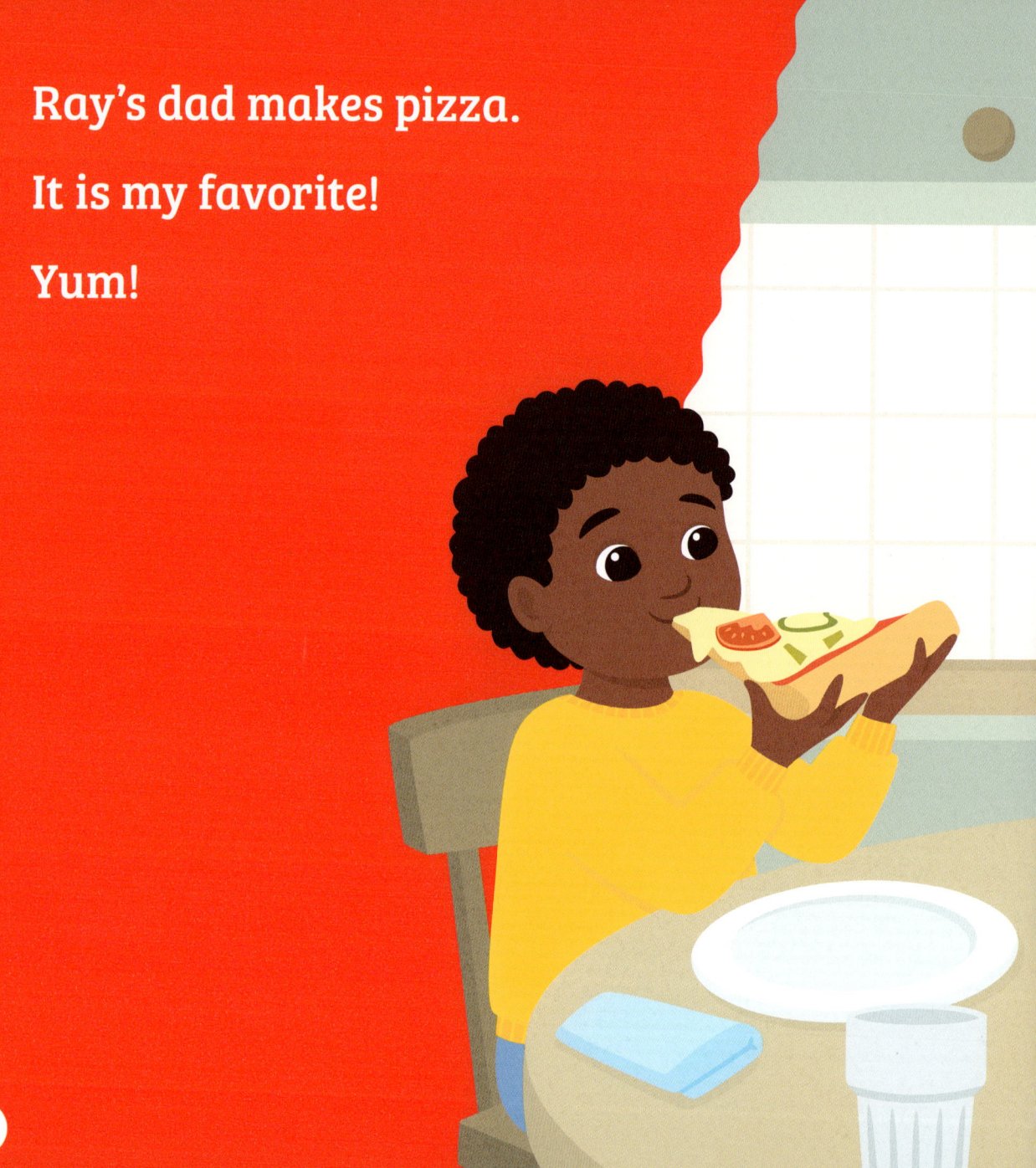

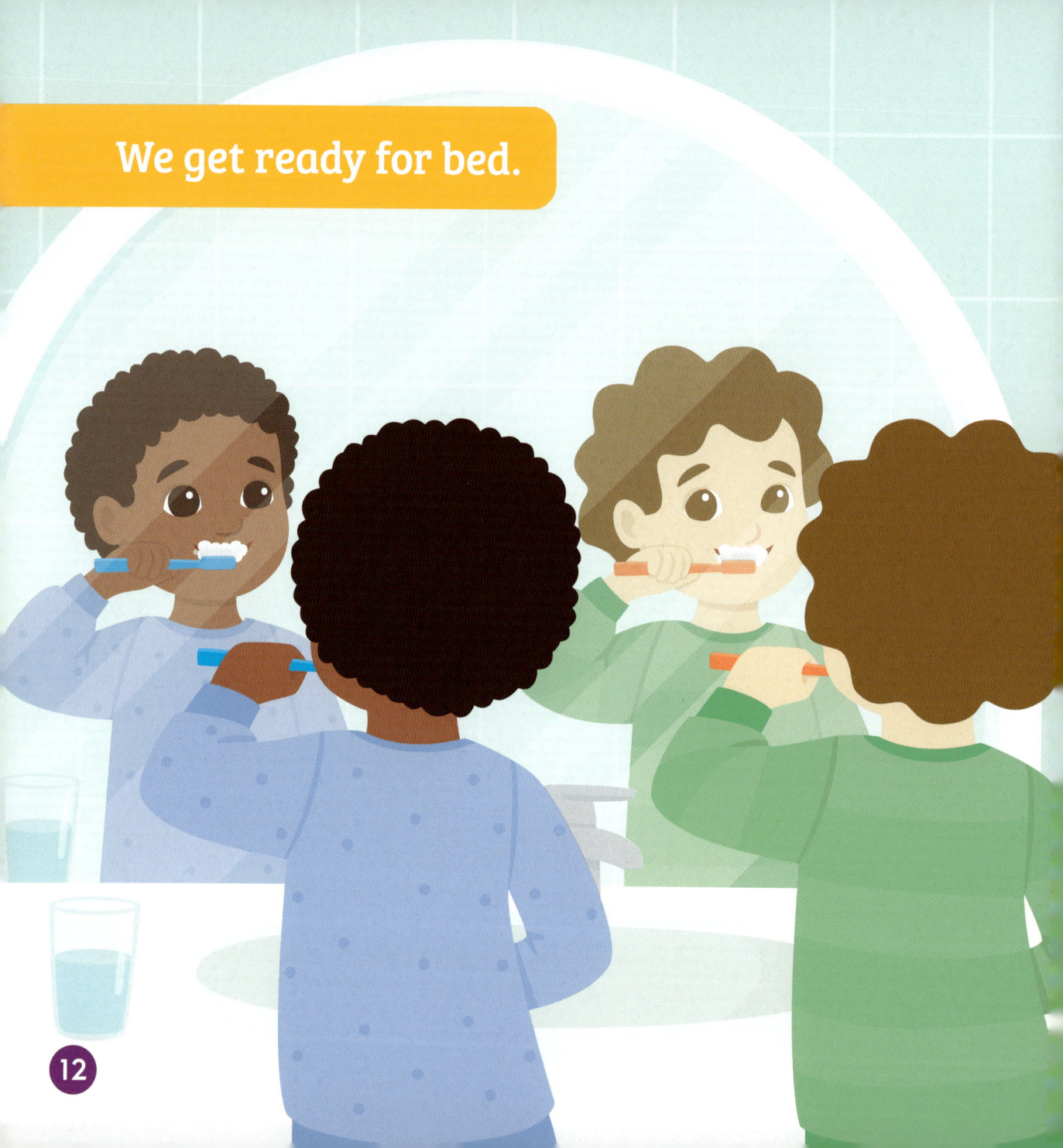

Then it is time to sleep.

"Can you leave the light on, Dad?" Ray asks.

I am glad he asked. I like the light on, too.

Mom picks me up in the morning.

"Did you have fun?" she asks.

"Yes!" I say. "When can Ray sleep over at our house?"

Let's Review!

What helped Sammy have fun and feel safe during his first sleepover?

A. He brought his own toy.   **B.** He played with a dog.
C. He slept with a light on.   **D.** He drank milk before bed.

Picture Glossary

excited
Feeling eager and interested.

favorite
The person or thing you like more than all the others.

pack
To put objects in a bag or container to move or store them.

sleepover
An occasion of spending the night away from home or having someone spend the night at your home.